FILTHY MAID

DIRTY BILLIONAIRE BOSS

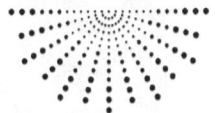

TALA MELTON

plicit Press
Erotica Fiction

GET NAUGHTY UPDATES

Click here or Visit
TalaMelton.com
for more Naughty Maid Stories

Filthy Maid: Dirty Billionaire Boss

Digital Edition 1 is Copyright © 2020 by Tala Melton. All rights reserved.

eISBN: 978-1-62327-712-3

Print ISBN: 978-1-62327-713-0

CHAPTER ONE

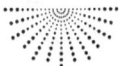

*H*er name flashed on the screen as she stood in front of her webcam, dressed in a black and white maid's outfit, iron in one hand, a wrinkled shirt in the other. She didn't say anything, plugging in the iron and unbuttoning the top button of her outfit, her beautiful breasts were now exposed just enough to get the attention of every man who logged on to the *'Filthy Maids'* website.

There were already two-hundred active viewers watching Ellie. Her name flashed across the bottom of the screen, encouraging viewers to tip her. She didn't mind using her real name, too, since it sounded like a fake pornstar name anyway. Her tip counter was still on zero, so she just ironed the shirt and ran her fingers across the top of her cleavage.

She had learned, in the few weeks that she had been doing this job, that patience was key. You didn't want to give too much away too soon. Tips were what got your clothes off, and Ellie knew this.

It didn't mean that she couldn't tease the men watching, though, tantalizing them with the possibility of seeing her naked so that they would pay for the privilege. She undid another button, and the tip counter started to rise. By the time she was down to just her bra and panties, she was sitting on $759. It had been a very good day.

The men watching her were, for the most part, just there to get their *rocks* off. They pulled on penises of all shapes and sizes, some of them with lube, some with Vaseline, others dry. Some of them had cum already; others were close.

Her cellphone was vibrating, a message alert. She ignored it, not wanting to be distracted. There were just five minutes left for the session anyway.

"We've had a strange request if you'll come into the office..." Wendy, the owner, and manager of *Filthy Maids,* said when Ellie finally answered her phone.

"What kind of request?" Ellie asked.

"I think you'd better come in..."

* * *

THE *FILTHY MAIDS* offices were in a trendy part of downtown. It took Ellie 15 minutes to get ready, and another half-hour to get there. New York was especially hot today so that by the time Ellie was seated in front of Wendy; she looked like she needed something cold to drink.

"So, I got a call this morning from someone who would like to remain anonymous..."

"...and," Ellie asked, really curious but also frustrated because Wendy just wasn't getting to the point.

"Can you clean for real?" Wendy asked.

"Huh?"

Wendy went on to explain to Ellie that a *very rich man* wanted her to clean his Manhattan penthouse. She explained to a wide-mouthed Ellie that she would be watched, but there would be no physical contact. She assured her that he had been vetted and that this was a legitimate opportunity for her to make a lot more money than she normally would.

"It will be like giving him a private lap dance in a very private, very trendy booth.." Wendy concluded.

"And all I'd have to do is *clean* his apartment?"

"Yes... It's quite a large penthouse, though, about 3000 square feet. Can you handle that?"

"Would I have to clean it all in one day?"

"No... You would just have to get completely naked each time!"

The way Wendy said the last sentence made it sound to Ellie like this might have come directly from the client. She wasn't sure about the full nudity, but she also needed the money. It was good pay for just a couple of days work, and just to get naked. Ellie still wasn't sure about this, just because there were more than enough horror stories about young women, recording devices, and the Internet.

"And you're *sure* about him?" she asked Wendy again, just to be sure.

"I am... But if you're uncomfortable, I'll let him know!"

"No, I'll do it. If you trust him, then that's good enough for me..."

Ellie left the office as soon as she was done with her ice-tea. She walked into the New York heat with more questions than answers. It really was fine, though, she thought. Wendy wouldn't send her to a client unless she had vetted him thoroughly. Wendy took her business seriously, but she also took the privacy of the girls she hired as seriously. Ellie went home to go through her closet to find something suitable for her penthouse cleanup.

CHAPTER TWO

*D*evon Chase's penthouse was everything Ellie had imagined. She walked into the space and immediately took her coat off. It was still extremely hot in the *Big Apple,* but the coat was necessary. It was still frowned upon in modern, civilized society to walk around dressed as she was under the *heaviness.*

She put the coat down on one of the bar stools in the kitchen and got something to drink from the fridge. The latex of the maid's outfit was sweaty and hot, but she knew that she was probably already on camera, so she went into character immediately. The cliché of her outfit slapped her sweaty face as she looked around the space. She really should have chosen something with a little more class.

"Hello," came a voice over the sound system. Ellie almost choked on her water and looked around to try and determine where the voice was coming from. "Make yourself comfortable, and *just act naturally.* You can just clean the kitchen and living room
today."

Ellie took another sip from her water and then bent down to load the dishwasher. The space was a *single guy who lives alone* dirty. This wasn't bad, and so Ellie knew she would need to be creative if she was going to fill the two designated hours.

Her eyes still moved around the large expanse as she tried in vain to locate the cameras. She couldn't. Of course, she couldn't. Being a billionaire meant that one could install expensive cameras and microphones that were completely inconspicuous. So while Ellie knew she was on camera, not knowing where the cameras were meant that she had no choice but to *act naturally*, not knowing which direction she should play too.

She dragged the vacuum cleaner to the living room and started on the wealthy Persian. As she pushed and pulled the vacuum cleaner, she undid two more buttons. Hers wasn't so much acting as it was just a natural response to the heat. She was getting very hot and couldn't find the air conditioner remote. Actually, she hadn't looked for it.

When she was done, she pushed the vacuum cleaner back into the cupboard and closed the door. Then she stood in the middle of the kitchen, reached underneath her skirt, and pulled her panties down to her ankles. She stepped out of them, leaving them on the floor before she started to wipe down the counter surfaces.

By the time she was done with the kitchen, the top half of her latex costume was around her waist, her bare breasts glistening with sweat. She still had no idea where to look, and this made the whole situation awkward. She looked around again, anticipating an instruction that just wasn't coming. So she just stepped out of the latex and stood in the kitchen, emptying the dishwasher, which was now done. Ellie, completely naked now, packed the dishes in the cupboard once she figured out where all of them went, stuffed her outfit and panties in her purse, threw the *still necessary* coat on, and left!

* * *

"YES, I followed the instructions to the letter..." she said to Wendy in the elevator down. He had given her just one instruction really, and she really did follow it. With no feedback, though, no tip counter on a computer screen to let her know she was doing a good job, she needed to know suddenly if *he* hadn't said anything about her *performance*.

"Nothing..." Wendy said. "He just transferred the twenty-five hundred!"

"I thought you charged him two thousand?" Ellie asked.

"I did... I think it's called *a tip*!"

After a quick stop at home to get changed, Ellie was back on the streets. She needed to find two suitable outfits, knowing somehow that her outfit had nothing to do with the generous tip. She thought of the penthouse, how the lighting filtered through the neutral tones of the curtains, and bounced off the perfectly balanced shapes and colors of the furniture. It really was magnificent.

Ellie found herself thinking what a man who lived in a place like that might like. He could, she knew, have any woman he wanted, anyway he wanted; and he probably did. So there must be something about the distance, the *just out of reach* nature of this interaction that appealed to him. So she knew that at the very least, she would need to give him a good *show*, a *worth watching worth the tips* show!

At last, she found what she was looking for. And it wasn't in a novelty sex shop or similar establishment. It was, in fact, in a store that sold cleaning apparel called, incidentally, *Merry Maids*. And what she found was perfect, she thought.

She chose two maid's dresses, an apron, and a maid's bonnet. And then, because she could afford to now, she went to the Victoria's Secrets store on *Fifth* and got herself matching underwear for the dresses, one beige, the other one black. Happy with the success of her shopping trip, she settled into a chair in the garden of *The Ivy* and ordered herself an ice-tea and a salad.

Again her mind was on her *private* client. Ellie wondered what he looked like. She remembered his voice, trying to match it with the many faces she'd seen in New York since she'd moved here. She came up with nothing, of course. How could you match a *strange man who paid twenty-five hundred to watch her clean his living room and load his dishwasher while taking her clothes off* with a man walking on the streets?

He probably never walked anywhere...

AFTER A COOLING SHOWER, she tried on her underwear. Then she tried on the maid's uniforms, both dresses with buttons down the front so that Ellie could choreograph a much more dramatic reveal. She threw the outfits in the washing machine and then lay on her bed, naked, her thoughts turning again to her mystery client. He was probably a millionaire, she thought. Or perhaps even a *billionaire*.

The raspiness of his voice lingered in Ellie's head for a long time. She fell asleep to "*act naturally*" playing in her head, as opposed to what, she wondered.

"He says 12 noon tomorrow..."

"Okay," Ellie replied.

"He says if you can do his bedroom tomorrow, the same like today, natural..." Wendy seemed to be having fun with this. She seemed to relish the fact that only she was in communication with the mystery billionaire who was paying to see Ellie naked.

"You're enjoying this, aren't you?" Ellie said at last.
"Oh, I am incredibly..."

CHAPTER THREE

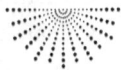

*S*he walked confidently up to Devon's building dressed in the beige dress. She had soft, comfortable pumps on her feet so that she looked like she worked in one of the city's *finer* hotels. She had, in fact, bumped into two women dressed similarly to her, whose name tags placed them at the *Waldorf.*

Ellie opened up the apartment, which wasn't locked, put her bag over the same stool that held her coat the day before, and tied her hair in a loose ponytail. She took the bonnet from her bag and tied it on to her head, pulling her ponytail through the back.

Armed with cleaning supplies, she made her way up the grand glass staircase to locate Devon's bedroom. It was easy to find, literally the whole of the first floor opening up to his sleeping space. *What wonderful dreams she could dream here,* she thought.

She stripped the bed bare, tossing duvet, sheets, and pillowcases in a crumpled heap on the floor. The temperature of the apartment was thankfully forgiving today, something Ellie appreciated. Her sweat from the previous day must have been clearly visible. She drew the curtains open, flooding the space with the noonday sun. She looked almost golden in the natural light.

"Don't move..." The same raspiness from yesterday.

Ellie froze. She stood still for an eternity before the instruction to *carry on* came over the high-quality sound system. She used a handheld vacuum on the entire mattress, taking her time, getting it as clean and fresh as the appliance allowed. By the time she was done, three buttons on her dress were revealing the matt black lace detail of her *VS* bra. She was pleased that she had made the purchase.

"Just there, don't move..." Devon was enjoying something about the way she had to lean across his *too large for one person* bed to get to the opposite corner. She was on all fours over the large surface, a deliberate move on her part, knowing that for the purposes of this exercise, simply walking around the bed would have been too *basic*. Again she was held in suspended animation for the longest time.

When she resumed 'natural,' she rushed downstairs to load the washing machine with linen, took fresh sheets from the hall cupboard, and went upstairs to tackle the massive task of making the incredible proportions of the sleeper. It was easier than she anticipated.

She sat on the just-made bed, took her bonnet off, and took her hair out of the ponytail. Ellie slowly undid the remaining buttons on her dress and let it fall on either side of her as she arched her back at an almost supernatural angle on the bed, her hands going far behind her, her breasts reaching majestically towards the sky. He didn't have to tell her not to move now. She just took a deep breath and held the pose, looking every bit like a *VS "Angel."*

"Wow," she heard, at last—a whisper.

She took her clothes and put them on the reading chair in the corner. Then she turned on the polisher, and after struggling a bit to get a handle on the huge machine, she moved it around on the wood laminate flooring, bringing it to incredible life. It had obviously not been polished in a while.

Nothing but her bra and panties on, and her comfortable pumps, she almost danced from one end of the room to the other, lifting dirt, laying down polish, and then stripping it to a splendid shine. Ellie had to admit to herself that she'd never enjoyed cleaning as much as she was just then. The massive machine fit into a cupboard she wouldn't have known existed if it wasn't for the list left by Devon for her benefit.

She walked over to where her clothes were. She bent over the chair, lifted her left foot, reached behind herself, and took the pump off. She repeated this on the right. Again this looked very *modelesque*. Still *VS*... *Burberry* even... Expensive, classy, very tasteful...

"You're killing me..." The voice was still a raspy whisper. Ellie enjoyed the feedback. It made it easier for her to do what she needed to if she knew what he was enjoying.

She lazed for a moment, looked around for what else needed cleaning. She was also wondering what to take off first, the delicate lace bra, or the almost absent panties. She decided to mix things up, brought her legs together, lifted them in a perfect pike, and pulled the black lace off her bottom. Then she parted her legs in a magnificent split, held it just a moment, crossed her legs, and resumed her sitting pose.

Ellie really was great at this, regardless of how she had doubted herself in the beginning. And, even though she still wouldn't admit it to anyone, she really enjoyed it. It was liberating, being two people in the same life. She could be a dedicated college student by day, sexy maid by noon. Everything her mother had instilled in her; all her augmented views on feminism and the liberation of female sexuality were now being applied in real life. She was literally being paid for being sexy.

She took the feather duster, a cliché she would have avoided if the room wasn't in terrible need of dusting, and she ran it across the many surfaces in the space. When she was done, she slid the handle of the duster under her bra strap, like an arrow returned pre-quiver, and she went into the ensuite bathroom. Dirty towels were on the floor, a piece of his underwear too, and so Ellie popped downstairs to throw this load in the wash. As she ascended the stairs, she really looked angelic with the feathers on the duster over-head. She couldn't have planned this better if she tried.

"Slowly... Please..." Devon was enjoying what he thought was a choreographed move on Ellie's part. He sat back at his desk, proud of himself for *choosing* her, almost as though he had created her himself.

She attempted a slow ascent, unsuccessfully at first, because she still had thoughts of his first instruction, to act naturally. What had changed? She was just settling into this gig, and now he was flipping the script. What was he doing?

At the top of the stairs, she realized, after feeling a slight tickle on the back of her neck, that she still had her bra on. She pulled the duster from its perch, *more sword than arrow* now, and just because the clasp was in front, removed the bra in a singularly sexy motion.

Completely naked now, she went to the chair, dropped the bra on the pile, and stood in the window, taking in the magnificent view of the city. Then she went to the bathroom again, got under the shower, and let the water wash away the effort and work she had done today. This really was quite a large penthouse, even if the cleaning was done in days. And she had to be sexy while cleaning?

It was worth it, terribly rewarding, but utterly exhausting...

CHAPTER FOUR

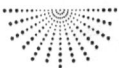

*T*here wasn't a protocol about showering. Ellie wasn't sure if she was breaking any rules, but she really needed a shower. She did wonder, as the water came down hard on her if the cameras extended to the shower cubicle. Unsure, she lathered herself with the manly scent of sandalwood, the only available shower gel.

One could, under normal circumstances, feel when you were being watched, right? Ellie felt, in the rest of the penthouse, that there was a *Big Brother* presence. Even in the bathroom earlier, in this very bathroom, she'd had the sense that she was being watched. In the cubicle, she was unsure. She hoped that she was, though, wanting suddenly to seduce her client out of hiding.

Was it possible, she wondered, leaning against the side of the cubicle. Did this man want to be seduced? Could he be?

These and many similar questions swirled around in her head, her fingers finding the soapiness on her breasts. She massaged the white lather to foamy mountains before letting the water wash them away down her front between her thighs. She was standing in a way that made the water form a clear river route from her neck to the beautiful place where her thighs met.

She listened, waited for the rasp over the audio system. Nothing. She thought of opening the cubicle, sliding the glass ajar just a little so that if the client was in the penthouse, the client would know that he could come it. Still nothing. She turned to face the wall of the cubicle and let the waterfall down her back, her one hand between her legs, touching herself in a way that wasn't obvious, but also *not obvious.*

After a while, she felt silly. Of course, there was no way that there were cameras in the bathroom. This was *his* bathroom, and why would he have cameras to watch himself? The short answer, he wouldn't!

She was already mid-shower, halfway to clean, so she just decided to finish up. She had already started to touch herself and thought of continuing, but since her two hours were up, she did need to get out of there, give the client his apartment back. Ellie let the waterfall on her hair all over her head. She gave herself one last lathering of sandalwood and then let the water wash the white away.

She stepped out of the cubicle and took a towel off the rack. She wrapped it around herself, and took the hairdryer off the wall, turned it on. She imagined that the client had hair if this appliance was anything to go by. There was nothing in the space that suggested a wife or live-in girlfriend. There was nothing that suggested any kind of girlfriend, in fact.

The hairdryer broke the silence in the space harshly so that Ellie was just now aware of how quiet it was before. She wanted her hair dry quickly so that she could return the space to its silent normal. It wasn't happening fast enough, though.

As soon as her hair wasn't dripping, she turned it off,

unable to take it anymore. She ran the towel over her body quickly and walked into the bedroom towards her clothes. Had she been looking, she would have seen him, but nothing said to her that Devon Chase would be in his bedroom in his apartment.

"Did you enjoy that?" he asked from the opposite corner to where Ellie's clothes were.

"Oh, I'm sorry... I didn't know you'd be back... I just needed to..."

"It's fine... I'm Devon..." He didn't offer her his hand, instead of letting her get to her clothes.

"I really wasn't sure..." Ellie continued, struggling now with her bra. She was a little distracted by how incredibly attractive the middle-aged man was standing in front of her. Surely he wasn't the client.

"I'm Ellie..." she said, finally succeeding to get her bra and then her panties on. She wrapped the maid's dress around her, buttoned it all the way, sat down on the chair, and put on her pumps. All of this happened in silence, Devon watching her every move.

"You look like a whole lot of fun..." he said.

"It's been said," she said.

Another long silence.

When she was ready to leave, she walked, passed him, and down the stairs. He didn't follow her, watching her leave instead. She grabbed her purse off the counter and walked towards the door. She turned around to see him still standing on the landing at the top of the stairs.

"I like watching you..." is all he said, and she left...

* * *

"I think I messed up..." Ellie's voice was shaky.

"What happened?" Wendy needed to know.

She proceeded to tell her boss in a little too much detail the sequence of events from the time she finished cleaning to the time she left the apartment. When she was done, Wendy said nothing. This was a day for protracted silences, it seemed. Ellie hated protracted silences.

"Aren't you going to say anything," she asked.

"There's nothing to say... He just tipped you *a thousand dollars*..."

Ellie typed *Devon* into her Google search bar as soon as she hung up the phone. She needed to know who this extremely generous man she had never seen before was, hoping to get some clue as to why he would be so generous. *Devon Chase* had several pages of results, so she just clicked on images. It was him.

She read an article about him in the New York Times online, a biographical piece on Mr. Chase, and Ellie was convinced that she knew who he really was. He was *Batman*. He had to be Batman, and she was to report to the *bat cave* tomorrow at noon!

In her own apartment, Ellie spent the better part of the afternoon looking at every photo of Devon she could find online. There was a hell of a lot of them. She started to touch herself several times and then stopped. There was something about pleasuring herself to thoughts of Damon while still in his employ that seemed somehow wrong.

There was, of course, absolutely nothing wrong with this. Ellie knew this. What was uppermost on her mind was that this act of self-manipulation might just leave her wanting, especially now that she had come face to face with the billionaire. He had seen her up close and naked, making no move to touch her, however.

She really wanted him to touch her, she knew, but all that played in her head as she now made her way to her own shower, to clean herself with her own feminine products, was what he had said to her as she walked out of his apartment.

"I like to watch you!"

She wondered as the hot water enveloped her, as the scent of lemongrass and lavender wafted up from the floor if watching really was all he wanted.

CHAPTER FIVE

*W*hen she walked into the *Batcave* the next day, a little early at around 11:30, she found Devon sitting in the stool that usually held her handbag or coat. She took a breath, and tried with all her might to hide all the thoughts she had had of him all of yesterday afternoon, and in fact until just that second when for the second time in as many days she had come face to face with Devon Chase.

"I promise I'll just watch," he said.

"Where would you like me to clean today," she asked, putting her handbag down on the counter next to him. She was wearing the second outfit she had purchased, the second beige bra and panties. Ellie couldn't wait to get down to these, knowing that if he had been impressed by the black, this set would literally light his fire.

"I think we'll do the library. That's the only other room in *desperate need* of a clean..." The way he said *desperate* and *need* together made Ellie very, very hot. And very, very wet!

She got the cleaning supplies from the cupboard and then

waited for him to lead the way. Walking behind him, her eyes were on his behind. She really could look nowhere else. Her mind was already going to places it had been before, and now he too was close enough for her to reach out and touch him.

Damon walked almost too slowly down the long hallway off the living room, almost as though he knew she was looking at him. He was giving her a show, it seemed, and this show held her mesmerized so that when he reached the library cum study cum office, she almost bumped into him because quite suddenly he just stopped outside the door.

"Sorry," she said, even though she really hadn't bumped into him.

He let her walk in first so that now it was he who was looking at her. She got started immediately, moving the already neatly placed items on the large glass table to one side. She leaned over the glass and started to wipe it, watching out of the corner of her eyes as Devon came round to sit behind it. He played with the chair for a minute, moving it back and forth, back so that his legs were visible, and then so close to the table that his legs disappeared underneath it. He found a comfortable middle ground and reclined into the high back, as comfortable.

Ellie moved the items over to the polished side of the surface, and then cleaned the other side, getting all her buttons undone so that the dress too quickly revealed her sexy as all hell underwear. Devon moved the chair under the table, surprised by how quickly he was sporting a full and firm erection.

She hadn't noticed even though her eyes were really more on him then on the table she was cleaning. She got it perfectly straight, every single item back in its place without really paying attention. Devon was fumbling underneath the glass, and she could see what he was doing despite her best efforts not to look. But she really couldn't take her eyes from where he was undoing his trousers, desperate to free his hardness from its prison.

He pushed back in the chair and pulled his trousers below his butt. Then he reclined back in the seat and let her look!

Ellie stood up now. Her head was filled with every reason why this should not be happening, but she was already taking her dress off completely. She kicked her pumps off and walked around the table to where Devon was moving thick fingers on himself already. She heard Wendy's voice in her head, although what she was saying wasn't clear. She heard the sound, definitely Wendy, but no words.

"We really shouldn't be doing this..." Devon said suddenly. Ellie stopped, unsure of how to proceed. "But it is too late to turn back now, right?"

Ellie got on the ground between his legs. She removed his hand from his penis, replaced it with both of hers, moved her fingers up and down the impressive shaft. Then she wrapped her mouth around the head and went down as far as she could. She brought her mouth up and down on him slowly, sucking hard on the incredible girth, determined to beat it into submission, determined to answer him without words.

"Right..." is all Devon said, over and over again, in his signature raspy whisper.

Then Devon stood up, taking her mouth with him for a minute before it had to be removed from him because he was too tall. He lifted her to her feet and pressed her against the side of the glass. Slowly he unclasped her bra, let it hang for a minute. Then he removed it completely. He got on his knees now, taking her panties the length of her legs and slipping them away from her delicate ankles.

She had very pretty feet so that Devon was momentarily distracted with them. One by one, he put every one of her toes in his mouth. Then he was kissing her ankles before he was again sucking sensually on all her toes, one at a time, and then all of them together, easy because her feet were really very tiny.

When he suddenly came face to face with her wet place, his mouth on her almost too quickly, the suck lick tonguing intense and intrusive, she literally almost fell over, saved by the side of the table. Devon grabbed her hips with both hands, held her firmly in place, and proceeded quite literally to devour her.

His mouth worked on her in a way that said he, too, had been contemplating this very moment for a while. He had, in fact. While Ellie was busy half touching herself yesterday, Devon brought himself to three orgasms in quick succession with just the memory of her naked in his bedroom to work with. It was really all he needed to get himself over. Now she was here, in the flesh, and try as he might, he knew it wouldn't be long before he really just needed to be inside her.

He stood up now, kicked his jeans off completely. He pressed himself up against her and brought his mouth onto her neck, and then onto her breasts. Then he was kissing the side of her face, desperate for her mouth but unsure. Ellie was the one who turned so that his lips were on her. It was she, in fact, who put her tongue in his mouth and let him do with it what he will.

Devon's fingers found the inside of her, carefully. He savored the slowness of the insertion, one and then two fingers, deep inside her. He was fingering her with the greatest care as his mouth did things to hers she had never experienced before in her life. Kissing was always a favorite for her, and she thought she had kissed in every wah that was possible, until now.

Slowly, slowly Devon tried and succeeded to insert three

fingers into her incredible *kitty cat*, fingering her in long strokes, warming her up to white-hot!

And then, when at last he replaced the fingers in her with himself, he let out a sigh of relief, happy that this particular maid really was as filthy, if not more so, in real life...

ABOUT THE AUTHOR

Tala Melton is an emerging erotica author of naughty maids and their billionaire bosses.

Readers: I want to expand a few of the stories to see where the characters can be explored further. If there are any of the stories that you would like to read more about again, I'd love to hear from you!

Visit my blog at Tala Melton Blog
Join my newsletter for free exclusive previews Tala Melton Newsletter
Follow me on Twitter at Tala Melton Twitter
Like my page on Facebook at Tala Melton FB

Sign up for Free Stories from Xplicit Press Authors
Xplicit Press Updates
Like Xplicit Press on Facebook
Follow Xplicit Press on Twitter

MORE NAUGHTY MAID STORIES BY TALA MELTON

www.ingramcontent.com/pod-product-compliance
Lightning Source LLC
Chambersburg PA
CBHW020815130626
46554CB00006B/2449